OAKLAND PUBLIC LIBRARY. CALIF. 94612　　　　　MONTCLAIR

W9-BSW-146

OAKLAND PUBLIC LIBRARY. CALIF. 94612　　　　　MONTCLAIR

J-PiC
Elkin
2010
035268899

Samuel's Baby

By **MARK ELKIN**

Illustrated By **AMY WUMMER**

TRICYCLE PRESS

Berkeley

Oakland Public Library
Montclair Branch
1687 Mountain Blvd.
Oakland, CA 94611

My thanks to Amy Novesky
for opening the door.
—M.E.

....

Copyright © 2010 by Mark Elkin
Illustrations copyright © 2010 by Amy Wummer

All rights reserved.

Published in the United States by Tricycle Press, an imprint of Random House
Children's Books, a division of Random House, Inc., New York.
www.randomhouse.com/kids
www.tricyclepress.com

Tricycle Press and the Tricycle Press colophon are registered trademarks of
Random House, Inc.

Library of Congress Cataloging-in-Publication Data

Elkin, Mark.
    Samuel's baby / by Mark Elkin ; illustrations by Amy Wummer.
        p. cm.
    Summary: Samuel announces during show-and-tell that he is having a baby
and soon his kindergarten classmates are expecting everything from twins to
puppies, but while Samuel teaches them how to hold and diaper a newborn, he
has some qualms about becoming a big brother.
    [1. Babies—Fiction. 2. Schools—Fiction.] I. Wummer, Amy, ill. II. Title.
    PZ7.E4266Sam 2010
    [E]—dc22
                            2009007548

ISBN 978-1-58246-301-8 (hardcover)
ISBN 978-1-58246-349-0 (Gibraltar lib. bdg.)

Printed in China

Design by Katy Brown
Typeset in The Serif and Clarendon
The illustrations in this book were rendered in pencil and watercolors.

1 2 3 4 5 6 — 15 14 13 12 11 10

First Edition

For my parents
and all the children in my life.
—M.E.

To big brothers and big sisters everywhere!
—A.W.

MONDAY MORNING it was show-and-tell in Mr. Donald's kindergarten class. Samuel was the last to share. He stood before the class and took a deep breath.

"I'm having a baby!" he blurted out.

"He cannot have a baby," Sophie interrupted, "because he is a boy. My auntie had a baby. Only girls have them."

"He is so having a baby!" said Marcel, who was Samuel's best friend. "I'm having a baby too, and it's right here in my tummy."

"I'm having twins," whispered Carolee. She was shy but did not like to be left out.

"Two babies! That's too much crying," said Marcel. "One baby will be loud enough—right Samuel?"

Before Samuel could answer, Mr. Donald clapped his hands. "My, how time flies! It's time for recess already! Get your snacks and jackets and line up at the door."

TUESDAY MORNING, five more students in Mr. Donald's kindergarten class were having babies.

"My goodness," said Mr. Donald during circle time, "it seems to be contagious."

"Samuel might be having one baby, and Carolee having two, but I am having three," Sophie announced. "My triplets are due very soon!"

"Well, look how big *my* baby is!" said Marcel. "You can feel its elbow."

"I'm going to call one of mine Mr. Donald," Carolee whispered to Terri.

"I'll need extra snacks today—one for me and three for my babies," said Sophie.

"I'm not having a baby," said Terri.

"Well, that's a relief," said Mr. Donald.

"I'm having a puppy," Terri continued, "and it's going to be a beagle. Listen closely—you can hear it bark!"

That afternoon in the play house,
Samuel, Sophie, and Marcel
practiced carrying babies.

"My mom says that rocking helps
when babies cry," said Samuel, "and
wrapping them tight like a burrito."

"What if the baby breaks all your toys?" Sophie asked him.

"Then Samuel will play at my house," Marcel told her. "I have plenty of toys."

Samuel seemed worried.

"Am I holding it right?" Marcel asked Samuel.

"You have to put your hand under the baby's head," explained Samuel. "My mom showed me how, like this . . ."

"When you have three babies like I will," Sophie declared,
"this is how you have to carry them."

ON WEDNESDAY after math, the students tried diapering their babies.

"Terri, that's not the right end!" Samuel showed her how to wrap the diaper around the back and through the legs.

Carolee was having trouble, too. Samuel handed her an extra diaper. "Each baby gets its own," he told her.

"And use both hands, Marcel."

"No way," Marcel said. "Diapers are stinky."

"Stinky?" Samuel asked. He hadn't thought about that.

BY THURSDAY, every student
in the class was having some
kind of baby, except Lawrence,
who had been out all week with a
fever. He quickly joined in.

"It's a goldfish!" he
announced proudly,
patting his tummy.

During free choice on Friday, even Mr. Donald was playing along. "Yes, boys and girls, I'm having something, too. Its name is 'One Big Headache'!"

The whole class was very, very busy. The students were preparing for the arrival of fifteen babies, one beagle, one goldfish, two hamsters, one kitty-cat, one stegosaurus, and a dump truck.

Samuel and Marcel were working at the art table.

"What color do you think my baby will like?" Samuel asked.

"Green," Marcel said. "It's my favorite."

"Do you think my baby will like *me*?" Samuel asked quietly.

"Of course. You're the best friend a baby could have," Marcel assured him. Samuel was not so certain.

THE NEXT WEEK WAS SPRING VACATION and students would not be coming to school. Before going home on Friday, Samuel told Mr. Donald, "I might have my baby by the time I come back. It's due anytime."

"Samuel, that's wonderful!" replied Mr. Donald. "Have a good spring break, boys and girls."

The week passed quickly and everyone returned to class—except Samuel.

"I received a phone call this morning," Mr. Donald told his students. "I'm happy to say that Samuel's baby has arrived."

"Yep, you can call me Uncle Marcel!" said Marcel as he strutted around.

"My babies almost came on the school bus," said Sophie.

"Mine are already playing peekaboo," added Carolee.

Just as the students were settling down, Marcel spoke up. "Listen!" he said. "I hear crying."

"Whose baby is it?" everyone wondered as they searched tummy after tummy. It wasn't Lawrence's goldfish. It wasn't Terri's beagle. It wasn't Carolee's twins or Sophie's triplets. The crying seemed to be coming from the hallway.

"Show-and-tell," called out Samuel as he appeared in the doorway. His dad was carrying a crying yellow bundle.

"This is Julia, my baby sister." Samuel was beaming.

"Let's gather in a sharing circle," said Mr. Donald.
One by one, the students brought out their babies
from under their shirts or sweaters.

Samuel's dad handed him his sister.

"Don't forget to put your hand under her head," reminded Marcel.

"Rock her gently," added Sophie.

"Look how teeny-tiny she is," said Carolee. "Samuel's baby is perfect."

"She does cry a lot," Samuel said. "And her diapers are really stinky." He rocked his baby back and forth. "But Carolee is right, my baby *is* perfect."

Soon Julia stopped crying. Little by little, her eyes began to close.

Then all the students in Mr. Donald's kindergarten class rocked their own babies to sleep.